A Beginning-to-Read Book

It's Groundhog Day, Dear Dragon

by Margaret Hillert

Illustrated by David Schimmell

NorwoodHouse Press

The **Dear Dragon** series is comprised of carefully written books that extend the collection of classic readers you may remember from your own childhood. Each book features text focused on common sight words. Through the use of controlled text, these books provide young children with abundant practice recognizing the words that appear most frequently in written text. Rapid recognition of high-frequency words is one of the keys for developing automaticity which, in turn, promotes accuracy and rate necessary for fluent reading. The many additional details in the pictures enhance the story and offer opportunities for students to expand oral language and develop comprehension.

Shannon Cannon

Shannon Cannon,
Literacy Consultant

Norwood House Press • P.O. Box 316598 • Chicago, Illinois 60631
For more information about Norwood House Press please visit our website at *www.norwoodhousepress.com* or call 866-565-2900.

Paperback ISBN: 978-1-60357-384-9

The Library of Congress has cataloged the original hardcover edition with the following call number: 2011038945

Manufactured in the United States of America in North Mankato, Minnesota
197N—012012

There is something I
want you to see.
Do you want to come
with me?

Yes, yes.
Where will we go, Father?
What will we see?

It is Groundhog Day.
The groundhog will
look for his shadow.
60

If he sees it, it will
stay cold for a little longer.
If he does not see it,
It will soon green up and be pretty.

Oh, look at this.
What fun!
What fun!

That looks like the one
I play at school.

This one is big, big, big.

Oh, what a funny one it is.

But where is the groundhog?
What does he look like?
Oh, I see him! I see him!
He is brown and little.

He is all the way out!
What will he do now?

Will he go in?
Will he stay out?

You guess he stays out, Father.
And I will guess he stays in.

He does not see his shadow.
He is out! He is out!

Now things will get green and pretty soon.

7

We can make Mother happy now.
We can get her something pretty.

What Father?
What?

Jenna's Flowers
Welco

No, no.
We can get Mother something green and pretty now.

Look at this one—
and this—
and this—

Oh here is the one we want.
Mother will like this one.

Mother. Mother.
Look what we have for you.

I see.
I see.
It is green and pretty
and I like it.

Here I am with you.
You do not see your
shadow, dear dragon,
so it is a happy day.

WORD LIST

***It's Groundhog Day, Dear Dragon* uses the 77 words listed below.**

This list can be used to practice reading the words that appear in the text. You may wish to write the words on index cards and use them to help your child build automatic word recognition. Regular practice with these words will enhance your child's fluency in reading connected text.

a
all
am
and
at

be
big
brown
but

can
cold
come

day
dear
do
does

dragon

Father
for
fun
funny

get
go
green
groundhog
guess

happy
have
he
her
here
him

his

I
if
in
is
it

like
little
longer
look(s)

make
me
Mother

no
not

now

oh
one
out

play
pretty

school
see(s)
shadow
so
something
soon
stay(s)

that
the
there
things
this
to

up

want
way
we
what
where
will
with

yes
you
your

ABOUT THE AUTHOR

Margaret Hillert has written over 80 books for children who are just learning to read. Her books have been translated into many different languages and over a million children throughout the world have read her books. She first started writing poetry as a child and has continued to write for children and adults throughout her life. A first grade teacher for 34 years, Margaret is now retired from teaching and lives in Michigan where she likes to write, take walks in the morning, and care for her three cats.

Photograph by Glenna Washburn

ABOUT THE ADVISER

Shannon Cannon contributed the activities pages that appear in this book. Shannon serves as a literacy consultant and provides staff development to help improve reading instruction. She is a frequent presenter at educational conferences and workshops. Prior to this she worked as an elementary school teacher and as president of a curriculum publishing company.

ABOUT THE ILLUSTRATOR

David Schimmell served as a professional firefighter for 23 years before hanging up his boots and helmet to devote himself to working as an illustrator of children's books. David has happily created illustrations for the New Dear Dragon books as well as the artwork for educational and retail book projects. Born and raised in Evansville, Indiana, he lives there today with his wife and family.